Dear Parent:
Your child's love of rea

D0000365

Every child learns to read in a differ
speed. Some go back and forth between reading levels and
favorite books again and again. Others read through each level in
order. You can help your young reader improve and become more
confident by encouraging his or her own interests and abilities. From
books your child reads with you to the first books he or she reads
alone, there are I Can Read Books for every stage of reading:

SHARED READING
Basic language, word repetition, and whimsical illustrations,
ideal for sharing with your emergent reader

BEGINNING READING
Short sentences, familiar words, and simple concepts
for children eager to read on their own

READING WITH HELP
Engaging stories, longer sentences, and language play
for developing readers

READING ALONE
Complex plots, challenging vocabulary, and high-interest topics
for the independent reader

ADVANCED READING
Short paragraphs, chapters, and exciting themes
for the perfect bridge to chapter books

I Can Read Books have introduced children to the joy of reading
since 1957. Featuring award-winning authors and illustrators and a
fabulous cast of beloved characters, I Can Read Books set the
standard for beginning readers.

A lifetime of discovery begins with the magical words **"I Can Read!"**

*Visit www.icanread.com for information
on enriching your child's reading experience.*

dragon

 snowball

 footprints

 snowballs

 hill

 snowflake

 icicles

 snowflakes

 map

 sun

 pond

 unicorns

 ponies

 wind

I Can Read!

BEGINNING
1
READING

my little Pony

Winter Festival

by Ruth Benjamin
illustrated by Lyn Fletcher

HarperCollinsPublishers

Winter had arrived!

There was snow

on the ground.

There were ❄ on the trees.

The 🐴 were getting ready

for the Winter Festival!

They were excited to welcome

the 🦄 to Ponyville!

The built an igloo.

They made

for the 🌨 toss.

They baked cupcakes

topped with ❄ .

They baked cookies

with snow-white chips.

The next day,

when the ☀ rose,

the 🐴🐴 were ready

for the Winter Festival.

But the 🦄 were not there!

"Where are all the 🦄 ?"

asked Scootaloo.

"I will look for the ,"

said Minty.

"What if they got lost?"

"I will help you,"

said Spike the .

"We can use my

to find the way!"

"Check the ice garden,"

said Spike.

He read the .

At the garden, they found

lots of and snow.

But they did not

see any .

"Look!" cried Minty.

"Here are in the snow!"

Spike and Minty followed

the to a big snowbank.

The were behind it!

"We found you!" said Spike.

"Did you forget about

the festival?"

"We remembered,"

said Rarity.

"We were on our way.

But we saw a pretty .

It was the prettiest

we had ever seen.

We watched the

dance in the ⌒ ."

"We followed the

up a ," said Rarity.

"Soon we were off the path

and trapped here!

We couldn't see the way back.

We are so lucky you

found us!"

"We are so glad you

are safe!" said Minty.

"My  will lead us back

to Ponyville," said Spike.

"Great!" said all the  .

"We promise not to run

after any more  !"

All the  cheered

when they saw the  .

"Now the fun can begin!"

said Minty.

Spike built snow .

Scootaloo made snow angels.

Rarity skated on the .

Soon the  began to set.

"This was the best

Winter Festival ever!"

said Rarity.